CHAPTER 1

When the Baron had arrived in the middle of the night, hovering outside Danny's bedroom window in the Morpho-Jet babbling on about Stonehenge, Danny had been sure as to what to do. It was the summer holidays so there was no school to worry about getting up for; both his parents were fast asleep and wouldn't miss him if he went on the adventure and his Aunt Maude, who looked after him during the day, was probably off somewhere hugging a tree and chanting.

In fact it only took Danny a couple of minutes to decide he was going to jump into the Morpho-Jet to help the Baron out again and that included getting dressed, leaving a note to say he was okay just in case he didn't get back before his parents got up for work and brushing his teeth. Who wants bad breath on an adventure?

Thirty seconds of ultra-speed flight after that...

"Here we are, old chap," said the Baron, leaping down from the Morpho-Jet, "Salisbury Plain, home of the ancient wonder Stonehenge."

Danny stood up in the open cockpit. "Where is it?"

"Just over the next rise, Templar. Wouldn't do to be seen arriving on a night time operation," explained the Baron, "element of surprise and all that, what?"

"I suppose so," agreed Danny.

"Exactly why are we here?"

"I'll tell you on the way, old bean, now grab the..."

Danny leapt from the Morpho-Jet, carrying the new rucksack that replaced the one that lay buried deep under the Egyptian pyramids.

"Thinking ahead Templar, first class," smiled the Baron. "Your training is coming on most splendidly." With that he pressed a button on his wrist watch and the Morpho-Jet changed appearance to blend into the surroundings. "Well," said the Baron slowly, "a barn is quite good for these surroundings, what?"

"Yes," agreed Danny touching the building with his finger which wobbled quite alarmingly. "But one made of jelly? And is that custard and cream on the roof?"

"Maybe, old chap," said the Baron shrugging, "but at the moment it's a trifling matter."

Danny winced at the bad joke.

"Anyway," said the Baron, "The old girl has done her morphing thing which just leaves me to get changed into my covert operations suit, what?"

"Covert operations suit?"

"Of course, old chap," said the Baron. "One would look rather foolish crawling around the English countryside at the dead of night in a safari suit, what?" He twisted a button on his khaki shirt. "Best stand back a bit old chap; this can get a little frantic."

Danny took a step back and watched in amazement as what appeared to be a tornado of blurred colour engulfed the Baron from head to foot. "State of the art instant wardrobe," said the Baron.

"Does it hurt?" asked Danny a little concerned.

"Not a jot, old chap," answered the Baron, "though the underpants change can be a little trick…OW!"

The vortex vanished to reveal the Baron in his new clothes. "What do you think Templar, old chap? This is the latest in operative technology, equipped for any eventuality, practically invisible to the naked eye in the dark. Impressed hey, Templar?"

"Er, is dressing like a giant, pink rabbit considered very covert in your organisation?" said Danny.

"Don't be ridiculous, old chap," scoffed the Baron. "That's why I'm wearing…" the Baron looked at himself and screamed, "…a giant, pink rabbit suit!"

"The ears are very realistic," sniggered Danny.

The Baron ignored him, threw himself to the ground and began to crawl across the plain.

Danny shook his head and strolled alongside the huge, snaking rabbit. "So why are we here then Baron?"

"Aliens, old chap," said the Baron as he dragged himself along. "A few weeks ago we started to intercept radio messages with our hyper-sensitive-interstellar-space monitoring equipment."

"Really," gasped Danny. "What did they say?"

"We're not sure, old chap," gasped the Baron. "All we could decipher were the words 'Operation Caravan' and some numbers. The numbers turned out to be a time, a date and a map grid reference but as for 'Operation Caravan' we're still none the wiser, what?"

"That's it?" asked Danny.

"'fraid so, old boy," confirmed the Baron trying to wipe off some sheep's droppings he'd just put his pink, fluffy paw in. "Which is why we are sneaking toward Stonehenge in the

middle of the night. Whatever is going to happen is going to happen here, tonight and very soon."

Danny nodded his head in understanding.

"There's the old boy now," said the Baron pointing toward the collection of standing stones. "Right, we need to get as close as we can to keep an eye on things but be very careful old chap, I'm sure these space travelling blighters will be on their guard. Booby traps and that kind of thing, what?"

Danny nodded his head again and crept as quietly as he could alongside the Baron but something was worrying him. "Baron?" he whispered, "I may be wrong but I seem to remember seeing a picture of Stonehenge in a book and it didn't look like this. It was more, I don't know, busted up."

The Baron squinted through his monocle. "You're right old chap. It looks like someone has repaired it. Do you reckon it's the same chaps that do the crop circles?"

"I doubt it," replied Danny. "It would take ages to move stones that size and I think someone would have noticed."

"You're right, old chap," agreed the Baron, his face turning very serious. "It must have been the space-Johnnies whose signals we've been intercepting. From here on in Templar we'd best be very careful, they are bound to have set up a security system and we don't want to..." The Baron stopped mid-sentence and tutted. "Look at this Templar, old chap, some people have no respect for the countryside at all. Fancy leaving this length of wire trailing across the ground, someone could get hurt."

"I don't think you should..." began Danny.

The Baron gave the wire an almighty tug with his paw and the night was lit up in a blinding flash.

CHAPTER 2

"Phrrzt guphz dingz!"

"I say, old chap," said the Baron looking rather hurt. "I know I made a slight error of judgement but there's no need for language like that, what?"

"It wasn't me," said Danny shrugging his shoulders.

"Phrrzt guphz dingz," said a voice from behind them.

Danny and the Baron turned around to see a small figure dressed in a silver suit with a mirrored dome of glass on its head. It was holding what was obviously a weapon of some sort in its hands. "PHRRZT GUPHZ DINGZ!" it said again.

"I'm sorry old chap," said the Baron before adding with exaggerated slowness, "me-o...no understand-o...the lingo...o."

The small figure in silver held up a three fingered hand of apology, then flicked a switch at the base of the mirrored dome that covered his head. "Is that better?"

"Rather," smiled the Baron. "Couldn't understand a bally word you were saying, could we Templar?"

17

"Sorry about that," shrugged the alien. "I'm always forgetting to switch the translator on. My name's Splatz, by the way, Trooper Splatz."

"Baron Fortesque-Smythe," said the Baron. "And this is Templar, pleased to meet you old chap."

"Likewise," replied Trooper Splatz. "Now what was I trying to say...Oh yes, PUT YOUR HANDS UP EARTHLINGS, ANY FUNNY BUSINESS AND I'LL TURN YOU BOTH TO DUST!"

"Right-oh," said the Baron as he and Danny raised their hands, "seems clear enough now, what?"

Trooper Splatz pushed and prodded Danny and the Baron toward the middle of the newly repaired Stonehenge. "Nice job you've done here, Splatz old man," said the Baron admiring the stones.

"No talking Earthling," said Splatz, "...if you don't mind."

"Don't worry Templar," said the Baron tapping the side of his nose, leaving a smear of sheep's droppings there, "I've got everything under control. Can you smell something?" he sniffed. "Anyway, as long as we're on Earth, we've got the upper hand, aliens not used to our gravity, what?"

Trooper Splatz pressed another button and suddenly he, the Baron, Danny and a circular piece of Salisbury were plummeting down into the ground at vast speed.

Danny gave the Baron a hard look. "We appear not to be on Earth anymore, we're in it."

"Don't fret, old chap," said the Baron, "there's always plan 'B'."

For a while Danny, the Baron and Trooper Splatz stood in silence as the descent continued.

"Nifty helmet thing you've got there Splatz, old boy," said the Baron suddenly breaking the quiet.

Splatz tapped the helmet, "Oh you won't believe how much easier it's made our job. Each helmet is interlinked with each other through a central computer system, any information a single trooper receives is instantly downloaded to all the others. No need for boring meetings and memos, we all know it instantly."

"Impressive, old chap," nodded the Baron.

"Not only that," continued Trooper Splatz, "but you can also access all operational systems with it; doors, transporters, weapons, everything. Well, everything except the vending machine in the canteen, that still only accepts the correct change."

"Baron," whispered Danny, "when you've quite finished, what about plan 'B'?"

"Wouldn't work old chap," whispered the Baron. "In fact I'm up to plan 'Y' and nothing fits the bill as yet, what?"

"You must be able to do something? Hasn't that rabbit suit got any special powers or anything?"

"It hasn't even got any pockets, old chap," sniffed the Baron. "And I could do with a handkerchief; I think I've caught a bit of a chill crawling in the wet grass."

"Couldn't you give him a rabbit punch or something?" asked Danny.

The Baron ignored the joke and said, "For your information old boy, I am a Master in the art of Pong Phew."

"Don't you mean Kung Fu?"

"No, they are similar styles but one requires a lot more baked beans to be performed correctly," explained the Baron. "And in a confined space like this I'm not sure any of us would get out alive. Talking of which, that awful smell is still here."

Danny suddenly had an idea and whispering as quietly as he could he said, "What about the rucksack?"

22

"Of course! The rucksack!" screamed the Baron excitedly.

There was a loud crackling 'FizzzzZ' and the rucksack on Danny's back fell to floor in a pile of blackened dust.

"Thanks for that," said Trooper Splatz lowering his smoking laser gun. "I knew I'd forgotten something."

Danny and the Baron looked at each other and exchanged 'I think we're in trouble this time' expressions.

Suddenly the Baron sneezed very loudly, "Sorry about that chaps, didn't spray anyone did I?"

Splatz leapt back and raised his laser gun. "What was that?"

"What was what, old chap?" asked the Baron sniffing. "That... that noise you just made?"

"He only sneezed," shrugged Danny. "It happens with a cold."

"A cold?" repeated Splatz slowly. "I think I heard that expression when I was younger. It had something to do with being sick if I recall, luckily for us we eradicated sickness centuries ago." The alien shuddered, "I'd hate to see what would happen if we started to...sneeze, did you call it?"

The platform began to slow and eventually came to a stop. A door opened onto a long metallic corridor. Splatz ordered Danny and the Baron to walk ahead of him.

"So tell me, old chap," asked the Baron over his shoulder. "What's this 'Operation Caravan' all about then?"

Splatz pushed Danny and the Baron into a room before replying, "I'm not authorised to talk about it."

The door shut between them.

"What now?" said Danny running his hands over the smooth door as he tried to find a way to open it.

The Baron however had his mind on other things. "It's just not cricket, old bean. Not authorised to talk about it indeed."

"No he isn't," boomed a voice.

BUT I AM!

CHAPTER 3

"I am The Mighty Phartz from Uranus," said the alien that stood before them.

Danny and the Baron looked at each other and burst into laughter.

The alien, who looked like a bigger version of Trooper Splatz but with a star badge emblazoned on each of his space suit's shoulders, got angry. "What are you laughing at puny Earthlings?"

Between the tears of laughter the Baron managed to splutter an answer, "Sorry old chap; it's just your name."

"What about my name?" demanded the alien.

"Well to be honest, it stinks," spluttered the Baron. "The Mighty Phartz?"

"From Uranus?" giggled Danny.

The Mighty Phartz from Uranus was not amused. "I bet you stupid Earthlings don't even know where Uranus is?"

"Yes we do old chap," said the Baron. Then he and Danny both said, "It's in the back of Ur-underpants," together before bursting into more laughter.

The Mighty Phartz touched a button on his helmet and the mirror finished glass domed helmet became clear to reveal what appeared to be a very large, angry looking, yellow brain with eyes and a mouth. "Well, for your information, in our language, 'Fortesque-Smythe' is very funny indeed. We often have to say, 'I'm sorry, you'll have to excuse me, but I've just 'Fortesque-Smythed', especially in elevators."

The Baron and Danny were getting their composure back. "I'm sorry old chap," said the Baron. "Didn't mean to be rude, what?"

"I should hope not," said Phartz. "Besides I'm sure you won't find it so funny when I'm towing your useless little planet into space."

"What?" barked the Baron suddenly becoming very serious,

"You cad!"

"I knew that would wipe the smiles off your faces," smirked the alien.

"You can't do that," said Danny. "Every living thing on this planet would be destroyed."

"It is of no consequence," replied the alien. "It's not the living things we came for or care about."

"But…" began Danny but the Baron stopped him.

"Quiet, Templar old chap, this is the bit where the bad guy explains his plan and gives us the advantage, happens every time."

Just as the Baron predicted Mighty Phartz began to pace and talk. "Many thousands of years ago we travelled across space to your stupid blue planet with the intention of plundering its natural resources but when we got here we found a very primitive race running about wearing rabbit skins." Phartz looked at the Baron, "I see fashions haven't changed that much."

"So why didn't you do it?" asked Danny.

"Well," said Phartz beaming with pride, "we came up with the brilliant idea of letting you lot do the work for us. We implanted some clever ideas into the simple Earthlings' heads, things like mining, the use of metals and how to grow sprouts, that kind of thing."

"Sprouts!" snarled the Baron. "That's dashed bad form...no, it's worse than that, it's downright evil Phartz."

"We do our best," Phartz grinned. "Then we set up a towing hitch, left you to it and went back home."

"So you helped mankind to evolve just to do your work?" asked Danny.

"Exactly," said Phartz. "And didn't you do a great job for us. It would have taken us much longer to plunder a planet this size, but you Earthlings are quite ingenious when it comes to making a right mess of things."

"Right," said the Baron taking a deep breath, "I've heard enough."

"What are you going to do?" whispered Danny.

"Don't worry Templar, I saw this is a movie once," said the Baron from the side of his mouth. "We capture their leader, take him hostage, escape unharmed and foil their plan. Watch and learn, old chap, all part of your training."

"But..."

The Baron let out a chilling war cry and launched himself at Phartz who didn't make an attempt to move, in fact he seemed to be enjoying what he saw.

"Tally Ho...ooooooh!" cried the Baron as he flew the air...and then flew through Mighty Phartz...before colliding with a rack of alien spacesuits that fell on top of him in a pile. "Ow," said the Baron softly from under the spacesuits.

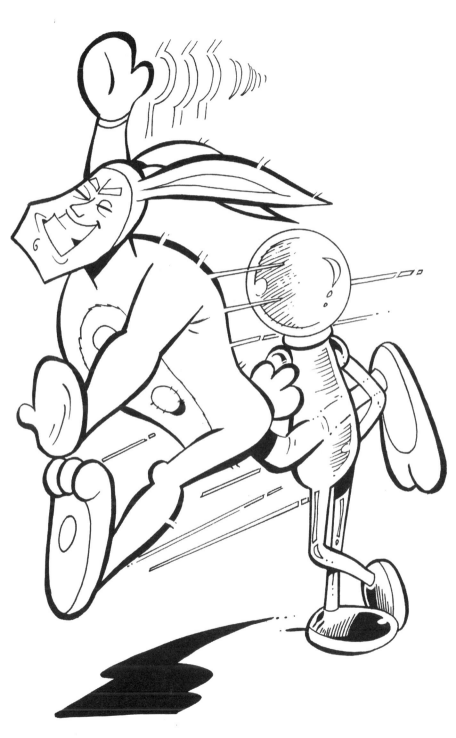

"Oh yes," chuckled Phartz. "And we made sure not to teach your ancestors the science of creating the perfect hologram, thought it might come in handy one day."

The Baron leapt up. "You'll not get away with this Phartz, you bounder!"

"I think you'll find I will," smiled Phartz and his image flickered and vanished.

The Baron slumped down. "Well Templar, old chap," he sighed, "that's it then. Earth will be towed off into space and 'ka-blam' the end for humanity." A small tear caught under the rim of his monocle before he burst into tears like a baby.

Danny shook his head and looked about. The room that held them only had one way in, or out, and that was secured by the locked door.

The walls were made from a smooth metallic substance as was the floor and ceiling. There was nothing at all in the room except him, the Baron and…

"Help me into one of these spacesuits," said Danny rummaging through the pile for one his size.

"This is no time for a fancy dress party," wailed the Baron. "We're all doomed, old chap. Doo-oo-oo-med."

"Not yet, Baron," smiled Danny slipping on a mirrored dome. "I played this video game once called 'Escape from Terror Island…'"

The Baron stopped sobbing and jumped to his feet. "Stop right there Templar, I know exactly where you're going with this old chap," he cried a huge smile on his face. "We both climb into a glass bowl alien helmet thingy and pretend to be goldfish and when they come to feed us we give them a nasty nip on their alien fingers and demand to be freed or we do it again."

"Er, no," said Danny slowly, still not totally convinced of the Baron's sanity. "Just do as I say and we might be able to get out of here."

Ten minutes later Danny and the Baron were sprinting across Salisbury Plain away from Stonehenge as laser bolts blasted all around them.

"Jolly good plan, Templar old chap," shouted the Baron above the noise of exploding English countryside. "I knew if I pretended to crack up you'd come up with something, it's all text book training."

"Really," replied Danny throwing off the alien domed helmet he was wearing.

"I particularly liked the way I allowed you use the buttons on the alien helmet to open the door and operate the platform to get us out," shouted the Baron zigzagging to avoid a blue laser bolt. "But my favourite bit of all was allowing you to pretend to be an alien guard and me your prisoner. I don't know how I do it sometimes, old chap, I really don't."

"Well, maybe next time we could just leave quietly without you stopping to thank one of the guards for their hospitality."

"I say old chap, won't do to be rude, what?"

The Baron pressed at his watch as they neared the Morpho-Jet, which wobbled back into its original form, raining hundreds of thousands of hundreds and thousands onto the damp grass, which is as hard to do as it is to say. Danny ditched the last of his alien disguise, dived into the cockpit and grabbed the control pad, closely followed by the Baron. Within seconds they had blasted off and out of range of the alien's weapons.

"Phew," gasped Danny. "That was close."

"It certainly was old chap," replied the Baron. "Though without my train..." his voice trailed off as he noticed something moving in the darkness at the back of the cockpit. "I don't want to worry you or anything Templar, old bean, but I think there's...something in here with us..."

CHAPTER 4

"I say Templar, old chap," said the Baron as he rolled past Danny on the Morpho-Jet's cockpit floor. "You handled the old girl a bit better last time."

"Last time," said Danny as the control pad was knocked out of his hand and the Morpho-Jet went into another spin, "it wasn't full of terrified sheep running all over the place."

"Good point," replied the Baron, skidding past on his

bunny's tail. "Still, it proves what a great blending job the old girl did if the barn disguise fooled these sheep into taking a look inside, what?"

"Marvellous," said Danny as he struggled to free the control pad from the teeth of a curious sheep.

The Baron managed to struggle past the sheep to reach his seat and sit down next to Danny. "Got any plans in mind, old chap?"

"Actually I have," Danny grimaced, trying to see around the sea of wool that blocked his vision.

"Jolly good show," beamed the Baron, "me too."

"I think…" started Danny.

"Me first," shouted the Baron raising his hand like a school boy. "We blast off to a remote desert island in the tropics, build ourselves a luxury wooden hut, live off mango fruit and coconuts and then come back when all this has blown over, what?"

"I don't think having the planet towed away by aliens is going to blow over, to be honest," said Danny through gritted teeth. He was struggling to stop one of the stowaways from chewing through

the wires of the satellite guidance system. "I was thinking of trying to find the alien's Mothership…"

"Mothership?" asked the Baron scratching his head between his long pink ears.

"A spacecraft that's the centre of their operation and big enough to tow the Earth away," explained Danny.

"I knew that," said the Baron pretending to clean his monocle. "I was just testing you, old chap."

"Of course," replied Danny. "Anyway, we sneak aboard the Mothership and sabotage their plans from the inside."

"Well done, Templar old chap," said the Baron replacing his monocle. "Exactly what I expected you to say considering the benefit of all the training I've been giving you, what?"

Danny shook his head.

"Good job the old Morpho-Jet is designed with space flight in mind." The Baron leapt from his seat and managed to shout, "Onward to the Mothership and victory!" before he was swept away by a woolly stampede. From somewhere at the back of the cockpit he added, "But first I think I'll secure our newly acquired cargo, what?"

"Now, that is a good idea," agreed Danny.

"Where is the bally thing?" sighed the Baron. "We've been looking for hours."

"Six and a half minutes actually, Baron," corrected Danny but he too was getting concerned. "They've probably got some kind of cloaking device hiding it."

"Make it invisible, what," said the Baron stroking his chin. "The prototype Morpho-Jet's used to have that...we lost six hundred of them before deciding on the morphing device instead."

"It's got to be here somewhere," hissed Danny, "we're directly over Stonehenge; it's the logical place for towing."

"Look, old chap," barked the Baron, pointing into space. "I saw something...there, a flash of light, what?"

"Could have been a shooting star," suggested Danny as they both looked intently.

"There it is again," exclaimed the Baron. "It's got to be the father ship."

"Mothership," corrected Danny. "But…"

"Give me the controls, Templar," said the Baron snatching the pad and he blasted the Morpho-Jet forward. "No time to lose, what?"

As they got closer Danny could see that the flashing in the night sky appeared to be some kind of opening, a brightly lit runway of sorts. "Baron?" he said uneasily.

"Shush, old chap," replied the Baron concentrating on operating the controls. "Nearly there…nearly there…splendid!" The Morpho-Jet landed on the metallic strip with a gentle thump.

"Right, we're in, let's kick some alien backside," beamed the Baron, "if they've got backsides of course."

The Morpho-Jet's canopy slid open. "All clear," whispered the Baron and he climbed quietly down with Danny following. "Do what I do and we'll be fine, old boy." He pressed his watch to allow the Morpho-Jet to morph,

which it did in its usual 'fashion'.

The Baron shook his head, his long bunny ears waggled. "Why a big plastic doll in a nappy sucking its thumb and moaning 'ma-ma' do you think Templar, old chap?"

"I'm not sure," admitted Danny, "maybe because this is the Mothership?"

Leaving the confused Morpho-Jet behind them Danny and the Baron sneaked across the hangar floor and slipped silently into a corridor.

"We need to find the centre of operations…" whispered the Baron over his shoulder to Danny.

"Maaah."

"…take control of the ship…"

"Maaah."

"…and somehow destroy Stonehenge."

"Maaah."

"Why on earth are you making those stupid noises Templar, old chap," said the Baron turning round. "Oh," he added as he saw the line of wide eyed sheep behind Danny.

"They must have followed us off the Morpho-Jet," shrugged Danny. "I thought you tied them up?"

"I did, old boy," blushed the Baron remembering he'd failed 'knot tying' classes three years in a row. "Still not to worry, maybe we can use them as a diversion or something later."

"Baron?" said Danny. "Don't you think this is all a bit easy?"

"Easy?" replied the Baron as they sneaked along the wall toward a door at the end of the corridor. "What do you mean old chap?"

"Well, when we escaped from their base under Stonehenge none of the shooting got even close to us really," started Danny.

"Obviously," dismissed the Baron. "Bad guys are notorious bad shots. I saw this movie once when there was a huge gang of baddies and one good guy right in the middle of them and..."

"Okay," interrupted Danny, "But what about us finding the Mothership? They can hide a huge spaceship from all the radar stations on Earth and all the satellites orbiting it yet they forget to shut the door on a brightly lit hangar. It just all feels wrong."

The Baron lifted his head and looked through a glass panel in the door they had reached and quickly dropped down again.

"We're in luck, it seems the head bad guy is just beyond this door and get this...

he's alone, jolly good luck, what? We're so close I can almost smell old Phartz."

Danny looked at the smear of sheep's droppings on the Baron's nose but decided against mentioning it; things were confusing as it was without giving the Baron too much to think about. "But," said Danny desperately trying to get the Baron's attention, "this all seems to be like the 'Taking of Space Station Alpha 7' game I played recently, everything you do is dead easy then suddenly it all turns out to be a tra..."

"TALLY HO!" shouted the Baron and he slammed his hand against a button that had a sign over it that read 'EARTHLINGS - PUSH HERE TO OPEN DOOR'.

The Baron, Danny and the sheep burst in through the door. "The jig is up Phartz, old bean," announced the Baron triumphantly. "I suggest you come quietly."

Phartz turned his head. "Ah, Fortesque-Smythe…"

Danny noticed a lot of wicked laughter from behind him and he turned to see the one time sheep, shape-shifting into a squad of brain-faced alien troopers all of whom carried mean looking weapons.

"...What took you so long?" finished Phartz. "We couldn't have made it much easier for you to get here."

The Baron straightened his monocle. "It's Templar," he said stiffly, "I'm training him and...well, he's not the quickest of learners, what?"

"What?" shouted Danny.

"Don't be too hard on yourself, Templar old chap," said the Baron patting Danny on the shoulder. "How were you to know it was a trap? I could have said something but you can only learn from your mistakes. It's just like that 'Taking of Space Station Alfred Evans' game I was telling you about, what?"

Danny could do nothing but stand there, his mouth hanging open in disbelief.

"Enough of this foolishness secure the Earth child and take Bugs Baron here to the Mind Melt Machine," ordered Phartz. "Let's get 'Operation Caravan', er…operational."

The squad of aliens grabbed the Baron and Danny and began to march them out of the room.

"I'd rather have a cheese melt," shouted the Baron defiantly at Phartz before turning to Danny as he was dragged along a different corridor. "Don't worry Templar, old chap," he yelled at his disappearing trainee. "I'll have this all sorted out in a jiffy, what?"

Danny smiled at the Baron but inside he was beginning to feel worried, very worried indeed.

CHAPTER 5

Danny found himself in a small room like the rest of the Mothership with smooth metallic walls, floor and ceiling. The entrance to the room was criss-crossed with thin lines of red light that buzzed quietly. As soon as he'd been put in the cell he'd tried touching the buzzing beams with the peak of his baseball cap, which had done nothing except leave him with a peak-less baseball cap and a feeling of helplessness.

"Well, that was stupid," he muttered to himself before adding, with a sigh, "The Baron's training must be starting to work on me."

Along one wall of the prison cell was a bed onto which Danny sat heavily in despair, things were looking bleak and not just for him. He was worried about the Baron, he didn't know what a Mind Melt was and although it sounded like the latest in roller coaster rides he had a feeling it wouldn't be that much fun. But above all that, he was worried about 'Operation Caravan'. Unless he did something soon, the whole world was going to break 'the longest distance travelled for a camping holiday' record by a good long way.

Danny smiled, despite his situation he couldn't help thinking that if the Baron were here now he would probably say something like 'I saw this in a movie once...' before shouting 'Tally Ho!' and doing something really mad.

Danny's smile suddenly got broader. "Maybe not a movie..." he muttered to himself. Quickly checking that the corridor beyond the buzzing red bars was empty he pulled the bed clear of the wall and chuckled at what he saw, "An air duct...just like in the classic

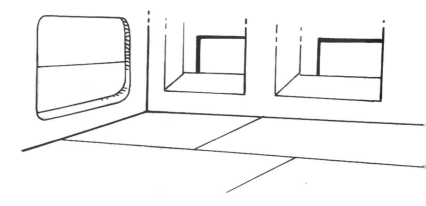

'Breakout - Prisoner 46213' game."

Working quickly Danny removed the grill and climbed inside the ducting tunnels. All he needed to do was find out where they'd taken the Baron and rescue him, but which way in this maze of rectangular ducts was it?

"It won't work you know old chap," echoed the Baron's voice through the metal tunnels.

"Right on cue," smiled Danny and he began to follow the sound of the Baron's protesting voice.

Meanwhile, in the Mind Melt room...

"It won't work, you know old chap," said the Baron as metal clamps snapped shut over his wrists and ankles securing him to the oversized metal chair he'd been thrown into.

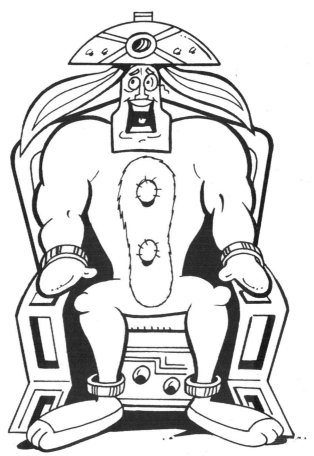

"Oh, really," droned The Mighty Phartz, "and why is that, Earthling?"

"Well," replied the Baron thinking as quickly as he could. "Firstly, you're the bad guys and everyone knows the bad guys always lose, old chap and secondly where are you going to get a tow rope big enough to pull a whole planet off into space, what?"

Phartz looked shocked. "Do you know what, you're right, I hadn't thought of that. My plan is ruined, curse you Fortesque-Smythe. Looks like the good guys win again; okay I'll come quietly and take my punishment without complaint." The alien raised his hands as if waiting for handcuffs to be placed on his wrists.

"I knew you'd see it my way eventually," smiled the Baron.

"Now just let me go and I'll see the authorities take it easy on…" The Baron stopped as he noticed the wicked grin on the alien's brain. "You're pulling my leg aren't you?"

"Of course I was Earth fool," spat Phartz visibly angry. "Do you see that metal helmet above you there, the one attached to all the wires?"

"Yes," said the Baron slowly.

"That is how we are going to get our 'tow rope'."

"I don't understand, old chap," said the Baron honestly.

"Obviously not," spat Phartz. "I wouldn't expect anyone from your backward planet to understand. But for one last time I will explain what is going to happen…and not because I'm the bad guy but because I want you to know what a sticky end you are going to come to."

"Actually, old bean," said the Baron swallowing nervously. "We don't have to go into details, what?"

"The metal helmet," began Phartz anyway, "will be lowered onto your head and switched on. It will then dig into the deepest, darkest corners of your mind and, as all forms of life are mentally in tune with their home planet, it will link your brain through the centre of Stonehenge, to the Earth's very core. This will form a magno-genetic bond that is stronger than any substance in the known universe and as we blast off into space, Earth will have no choice but to be dragged along behind us."

"That doesn't sound too bad to me, old boy" said the Baron.

"Look at it this way, by the time we have towed your planet across millions of miles of space to orbit around Uranus...no jokes!" demanded Phartz as the Baron's mouth began to open, "your mind and body will be so drained of energy you will look like a dried out prune...well, a dried out prune in a very large rabbit suit to be exact."

"I quite like prunes, what?" said the Baron putting on a brave face, which he had decided would be better than the wrinkly, squashy one he had just been promised for the near future.

"Enough of this bravado," barked Phartz.

"Begin the Mind Melt!"

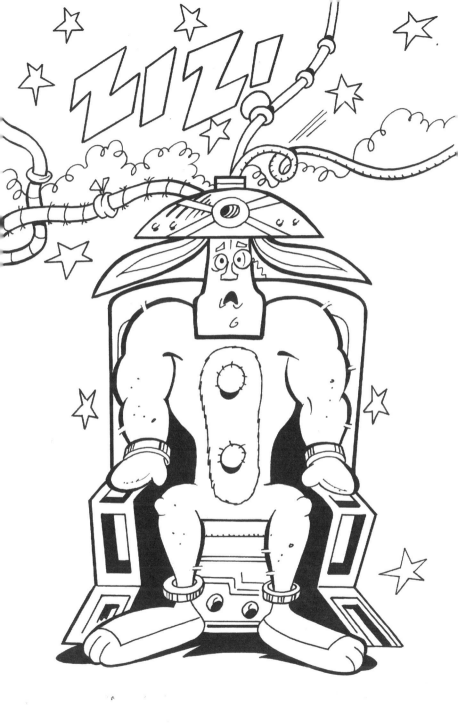

The alien trooper that was sitting in front of a huge bank of controls began to push buttons and throw switches and the metal helmet dropped onto the Baron's head, squashing his rabbit ears flat to his head. There was a low humming as the machine began to tap into his brain waves, then suddenly it stopped and the hum died away.

"What's happening?" demanded Phartz.

The trooper turned from the controls. "Er…it appears his brainwaves aren't that strong. They're more like brain-ripples to be honest."

"Is the Mind Melt on full power?"

"No, sir," replied the trooper. "But if we do that we could melt his brain before we get the planet anywhere near Uranus."

"Full Power!"

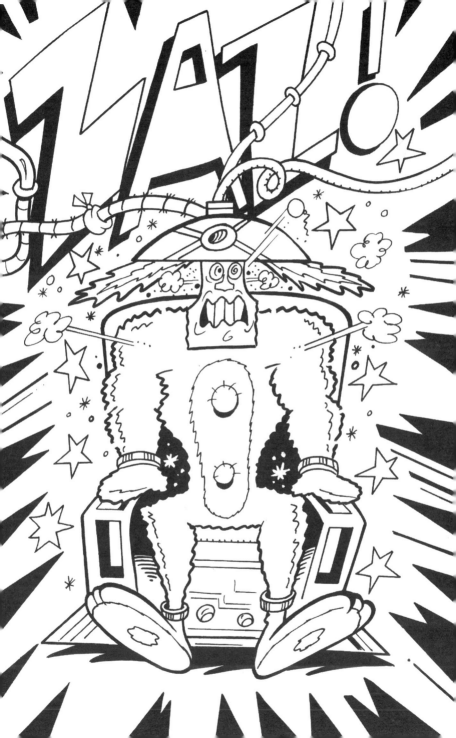

"We can always use the other Earthling once we've dried this fool out," added Phartz.

"I say," said the Baron, "you can't use Templar, that's jolly bad form he's only just started his trainin...g...g...g." The Baron was silenced as the Mind Melt buzzed back into life, this time digging far deeper into his brain.

Phartz looked at the viewing screen and saw a huge beam of light explode from the Mothership to link up with Stonehenge far below.

"Start the engines," he ordered. "Let's get this show on the road. Oh, by the way, did you remember to fit the towing extensions onto the wing mirrors?" The trooper nodded his head. "Good, let's go then."

The Mothership began to rattle and creak as the huge engines fired up and took the strain ready to tow Earth off into deepest space.

Suddenly there was a clattering of metal, a thud, quite a few crunching noises and lots of sparks and 'fizzing' as Danny dropped out of the air duct to land onto the Mind Melt control panel.

Outside the Mothership the beam of light was cut off.

"You!" screamed Phartz. "How did you..?"

"The air ducts," smiled Danny. "You've never played 'Prisoner 462I3' I take it, Phartz?"

"No I haven't but to be honest I'm actually more concerned why there are air ducts in the Mothership at all when we don't breathe air!" screamed Mighty Phartz. "I knew we should never have let those stupid TV designers from 'Changing Spaceships' on board!"

"Well done Templar, old bean," cried the Baron, free from the Mind Melt's influence once again.

"Get the Earth child!" ordered Phartz.

"Actually, sir," said the trooper operating the Mind Melt. "I think we have a bigger problem."

"A bigger problem?" spat Phartz.

"We've lost the towing link, I'm running out of patience and my beautiful Mothership is infested with free range Earthlings! How can we have a bigger problem?"

"It appears the Earthling critically damaged the central computer systems when he fell on the control panel," said the trooper nervously.

"So what?!"

"It's running in reverse, sir. The Earthling's brain waves are being absorbed by the computer through the Mind Melt mechanism."

"Wh-what?!" stuttered Phartz in rage before barking out, "Computer! Status report!"

"Love to, old chap," answered an electronic voice in reply. "But you're the bad guys and it would be jolly bad form if I was to help you out with your plans, what?"

CHAPTER 6

The metal restraints holding the Baron's wrists and ankles sprang open. "Thanks computer," said the Baron bounding free from the Mind Melt chair.

"No problem, old chap," replied the computer as Phartz frantically pressed buttons on the control panel in an attempt to regain control of the Mothership.

"What now, Baron?" asked Danny.

"Not too sure, old chap," mused the Baron. "Computer, have you got any plans, what?"

"Well, old man," replied the computer slowly. "How about I give you ten minutes to get back to your craft before I take these rotters off into a jolly far away part of the universe and keep them there until they've learned the error of their ways, what?"

"Sounds splendid, old chap," beamed the Baron.

"It does, doesn't it?" agreed the computer. "I'm getting a funny feeling that I saw it in a movie once," added the electronic voice. "But I've never even been to the cinema, what?"

"There you go Templar, old chap," smiled the Baron. "That's our plan."

"Get a move on chaps, you've only got nine and half minutes to get away before I blast off to Quadra-a-a-a-a-a-ACHOO!" sneezed the computer. "Sorry about that, I appear to have caught your cold, old chap."

The Baron looked embarrassed. "I do apologise, old chap...er, old computer...still I'm sure you've had worse viruses."

Danny and the computer groaned. "Any more bad jokes like that and I'll take you with us, what?" warned the electronic voice.

"Right-oh," grinned the even more embarrassed Baron. "Ready?"

Danny nodded and he and the Baron ran off as an alarm began to howl and the computer warned, "Deep space hyper-jump, nine minutes and counting, secure all loose cargo...and don't forget your toothbrush, what?"

Danny and the Baron ran down corridors, round corners, through control rooms, canteens and sleeping quarters and down yet more corridors.

"Deep space hyp-a-a-a-ATCHOO! (sniff) jump, six minutes and counting, what?" warned the computer over the Mothership's communication system.

"Do you know where we're going?" shouted Danny over the sound of the still howling alarms.

"Of course old chap," replied the Baron trying hard to hide the worried look on his face.

"Straight down the corridor, second door on the left, old boy," said the computer.

"Straight down here, second on the left," repeated the Baron. "You really should have more faith in me, Templar old bean."

Danny and the Baron sprinted down the corridor and burst into the hangar that was second on the left to be greeted by the welcome sight of the Morpho-Jet, which had changed its mind and was now a large pram...and the not so welcome sight of Phartz and twelve of his brain-faced alien troopers. "Going somewhere?" sneered Phartz menacingly as his troopers aimed their weapons at the Earthlings.

"Any chance of a little help here, computer?" said Danny into the air of the hangar.

"Certainly old chap," replied the computer cheerfully and just as the aliens pulled the triggers on their mean looking guns it added. "Weapons systems off line (sniff)."

There followed a lot of clicking and alien troopers looking at their useless guns. Mighty Phartz let out an angry scream.

"No matter," he hissed. "My troopers are all trained in the deadliest martial art in the universe."

"In that case I have two questions," said the Baron. "Is it Pong Phew and do baked beans have any effect on Uranus?"

"No it isn't Pong Phew!" raged Phartz. "Enough! Get them!"

The alien troopers dropped their weapons and began to make all kinds of weird movements with their arms and legs to go with the even more weird howls and whooping yelps they were letting out.

"I don't think I can take all these on, old chap," whispered the Baron, "even if I had a full stomach of beans. I'll hold them off as long as I can, you run to the old Morpho-Jet and escape."

"I can help," offered Danny.

The Baron gave Danny a huge smile full of pride. "You've done enough already Templar, old bean. Infiltrated an alien Mothership, rescued me from the Mind Melt, not to mention saved the world from destruction for a second time, what?"

"Listen," insisted Danny, "I've had a lot of experience with computer viruses crashing my games, I can help, I know I can!"

The Baron let out a sigh, "No Templar, the situation is lost, you must save yourself...but should anyone ask about this day just say a decent chap did his duty, that's all I ask...and maybe a statue in every park in the land...and a life sized portrait in every museum...and..."

"Remember Splatz told us about the helmets," interrupted Danny, "And how they're all linked up through the central computer? Well, when we first met Phartz he knew your name, we never told him it, he just knew it. It was Splatz who knew your name and his helmet must have fed that information into the computer which then passed it onto Phartz through his helmet. They are all linked together, what one gets they all get."

"Yes," agreed the Baron trying to keep up. "So...?"

"So how's your cold?" asked Danny.

"Well, I don't like to complain, old chap but..." began the Baron.

"Computer!" shouted Danny.

"Yes, old chap?" replied the electronic voice.

"Download 'Fortesque-Smythe' virus to all systems."

For a few moments the computer said nothing then, "Virus (sniff) downloaded...deep space hyper-jump two minutes and

counting."

The Baron looked at Danny in undisguised puzzlement. "I don't want to seem ungrateful,

what? But how did that help our situation?"

"They may have cured all sickness on their planet but not the

ones on ours," explained Danny, "so I reckon right about now…" he pointed to the alien troopers who were

advancing menacingly, a bit like angry ballerinas with fleas in their tutus. Suddenly one of the troopers stopped his weird howling and gyrating and went something like this, "W-a-a-a-a-a-a-a-a-ATCHOO!" instead.

As he sneezed a huge ball of snot exploded across the inside of his helmet completely robbing him of his vision. He ran round in utter panic screaming, "I can't see! I can't see!" until he collided with a metal pillar and knocked himself out.

"Brilliant plan!" laughed the Baron as one by one the alien troopers were blinded by great explosions of yellow, snot smearing across the inside of their domed helmets. "They've caught my cold...or virus...or both! Glad I let you think of it, old chap."

Danny had expected that but he shook his head nonetheless. "Come on Baron," he shouted, "let's get out of here."

"Deep space hyper-jump thirty seconds and counting, all aboard who's going aboard, what?" added the computer.

Dodging their way around Phartz and the alien troopers as they flailed around wildly, either bouncing off the walls of the hangar or beating each other up, Danny and the Baron leapt aboard the Morpho-Jet and prepared for take off.

"Deep space hyper-jump ten seconds and counting," warned the computer. "Nine...eight...seven..."

Danny hurled himself into the pilot's seat and jammed his thumb onto the control pad.

"...three...t-t-t-t-t-CHOO!...one. Deep space hyper-jump initiated. Toodle-pip, old chaps."

There was a loud whooshing and a blurred streak of light as Phartz, his alien troopers and the Mothership blasted off into the darkest region of space to begin their long exile and 'How to be Nice Little Aliens' lessons.

"I say, that was close Templar, old chap," said the Baron straightening his rabbit ears.

"Sure was," agreed Danny looking down on the Earth. "Fun, though."

"Did you see the look on Phartz's brain, old boy, when all his chaps started to fight each other, their helmets covered in liquid bogey?" laughed the Baron.

"Yeah, that was funny," agreed Danny and he and the Baron laughed for a good long while about that.

"Isn't the Earth amazing from up here," said Danny gazing at the blue and green sphere below them.

"The Earth is amazing from down there too," smiled the Baron. "That's why I do this job, I want it to stay that way, what?"

"I couldn't agree more," nodded Danny.

"Chin-chin old bean, the sun's starting to rise, best get you home Templar," noted the Baron.

"I suppose so," said Danny a little disappointed.

"One thing still worries me though, old chap," said the Baron seriously, "we didn't figure out where that awful smell is coming from?"

"Poo nose?" shrugged Danny smiling as he steered the Morpho-Jet back into the Earth's atmosphere and toward home.

EPILOGUE

Danny spent the next few days after helping to defeat the alien invasion kicking about his house and trying to avoid Aunty Mabel whose new hobby was spaghetti knitting. The clothes she made were just as embarrassing as the ones she used to make out of wool but at least Danny could eat his way out of them now.

The TV news had been full of the mysterious rebuilding of Stonehenge and how two crop circle makers, U. R. A. Nutter and I. M. Crazy, had claimed responsibility though Danny suspected it was because their new book, 'They're Not Crop Circles–

They're Very Good', was due out soon.

Just as things were getting back to boring normality Danny opened the door to find a five foot high steam powered penguin uni-cycling round and round his front garden. Dangling from one of its pumping legs was a very familiar wrist watch.

Danny grabbed the watch from the passing penguin and checking round for any witnesses pressed the button, at once the Antarctic antique curiosity changed back into the Morpho-Jet, its canopy wide open to reveal an empty cockpit.

Danny climbed inside and noticed a red light flashing, he pressed the button above it and a screen flickered into life showing the Baron's very worried and out of focus face.

"Templar, old chap" began the recorded video message. "Under attack...ninjas...Okinawa...need help...what?"

Then the screen went blank...

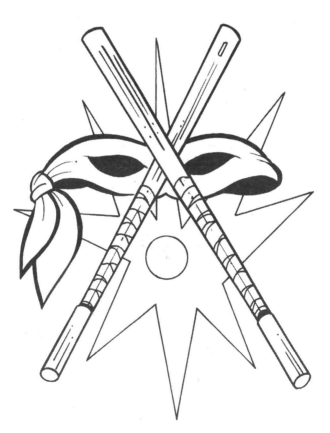

Printed and bound in Great Britain by William Clowes Ltd, Beccles, Suffolk